This book is dedicated to the 200+ people
who helped to create the story!

WHAT COLOR WOULD YOU MAKE VINNY?

Download the FREE
Vinny the Soccer Playing Dinosaur
coloring pages!

www.brandoncullum.com/vinny-color

Meet this green dinosaur.
His name is Vinny.

He plays soccer with his brothers.
But he is small and skinny.

Lenny on defense,
Theo and Charlie on attack.

Vinny plays goalie
all the way in the back.

It is the first game of the season.
The score is tied three-three.

The other team has the ball,
heading straight for Vinny.

0:06

0:05

0:04

The ball was kicked hard and square.

0:03

0:02

0:01

Vinny flew into the air.

The other team: Four
Vinny's brothers: Three.

The game was over,
Vinny's brothers are angry.

Vinny went home.
Not sure what to do.

What his brothers just said,
must be true.

Vinny saw his ball
and kicked it as hard as he could.

"I'm done with this game.
I'm leaving…for good!"

Vinny leaves his house
And looks for a place to sleep.

This was too high.
That was too steep.

He can not reach the grass,
no matter how hard he tries.

He lays on the ground
and begins to cry.

An old sabertooth appears.
He watches from afar.

He has seen Vinny play.
He could become a star.

Suddenly, Vinny sees a ball
flying from a distance.

He catches it and passes it back,
All in an instance.

"I've never seen a dinosaur
who can play like you."

"Stay with me and we will see
what you can do!"

Vinny stays with the old tiger and trains a lot.

Vinny trains when it was cold.
And when it was not.

They trained on the left
during the middle of the night.

They train during the day,
all the way on the right.

"There is one more thing to learn,
To make you great."

"You can't play tall, you are tiny.
That is your fate."

"You might be tiny,
but I am more."

"You can become great,
because I became........

Pele-a-saur's work is done.
All his lessons rang true.

Vinny must prove himself,
and show what he can do.

Vinny leaves his teacher,
and makes his way back.

He is going to find his brothers,
And rejoin the pack.

It is the final game.
The score is two-two.

Bill broke his foot.
He is hurt and through.

The referee announces
they will lose today.

The T-Rex team will win,
Unless someone else can play.

"They won't lose,
I can play on attack!"

The brothers are shocked.
Vinny is back.

"We have no other choice,
We have to put him in.

You better not mess up,
We can't lose again."

The game starts.
Vinny steals the ball.

He goes past one defender
and then past them all.

Flying through the air,

past the goalie with a roll.

The ball goes in.

Vinny!

Vinny!

Vinny!

Vinny is lifted into the air.
He is the hero of the game.

Vinny!

The crowd chanted Vinny!
Everyone knew his name!

Later Vinny was asked,
"Where did you learn to dribble the ball?"

With a grin Vinny answered,
"You wouldn't understand."

"You are too tall."

Can anyone teach him a Lesson?

Find out in....

ALFRED
THE TIME TRAVELING
DINOSAUR

Brandon Cullum and Friends

Made in the USA
San Bernardino, CA
14 October 2018